WISHBONE BILLY

Stephen Fitzsimons

CONTENTS

MEET THE PARENTS

Mr and Mrs Slurb waddled down the busy Wood Green high street, clearing a path with their great wobbling bulks. Each step they took resulted in a wave-like movement as their flesh rippled down from their thick necks until it crashed at their enormous bottoms.

During this waddling, rippling, crashing motion, the pair used their great, fat fists to stuff extra-large burgers (with extra mayo, topping and burger, of course) into their cave-like mouths. Mr Slurb snuffled a deep, wheezy breath of burger and dripping mayo, slowly turned around the large, neckless dome of his head and yelled (spitting pieces of burger on an unfortunate passer-by) 'Billy, get a move on you lazy brat! Do we have to do everything?! Keep-up! Your mother will miss her TV programme!'

'Yes, dad,' gasped Billy, who in his hands did not have a burger or even a small chocolate bar treat but instead EIGHT bags of food shopping that he struggled to carry. The plastic handles of the over-loaded bags had begun to cut deep into his hands, pressing on the bone beneath, whilst turning his fingers an interesting purplish-red.

'You're such a lazy brat,' added Mrs Slurb with an equally distasteful shower of burger spit. 'I don't know how your dad puts up with it coz it's driving me mad,' she concluded with a purposeful bite of her burger to control herself over the dreadful behaviour of her child.

After much waddling, rippling and crashing, the Slurbs eventually arrived at the bottom of Ringwald Road which was just off the main street. It was a pleasant enough place with terrace houses climbing a gentle hill with neatly trimmed hedges, freshly watered flower baskets and recently painted doors. All, that is, except number seventeen. This was the house of the never-cut hedge, the never-watered flowers, the never-painted door: it was the house of the never-done. This was the house of the Slurbs.

At the bottom of Ringwald Road, Mr and Mrs Slurb were leaning against a wall, huffing and puffing. On almost any Saturday, at this point, they would do this at the terrifying thought of having to stagger up the slight hill, pass eight *whole* houses, to their door. The thought of this terrible journey put the parents in a foul mood.

'You ungrateful little toad,' rasped Mr Slurb at his son who had just struggled around the corner carrying the eight FULL bags of shopping. 'Look at your poor mother all pasty like a fish. How could you be so selfish as to not help her up this hill?'

Billy stood silent and waited. He knew what to expect next.

'You miserable slug,' gasped Mrs Slurb as she tried to catch her breath. 'Look at what you've done to your poor father. He's as white as a cod with worry for me. You'll drive us to an early grave.'

Billy stood silent and waited; the bags cutting deeper into his hands.

'Well, don't just stand there you slimy maggot. Get up that great hill, drop the shopping off, and come back and help us,' said Mr Slurb rasping loudly.

'And be quick about it,' added Mrs Slurb gasping loudly.

Billy struggled up the hill with the shopping, pass the Slurb's broken front gate, put down four of the bags of shopping and desperately fumbled with his throbbing fingers in his front pocket for his key. Painfully, he turned the key in the rusty lock and pushed open the door. He picked up the four bags and stumbled pass the sofa and armchairs, past the dining table, to the kitchen where he gratefully deposited the shopping on the floor. Spending no time to rest, Billy went down the hill, and then up the hill again helping his mother to a brown armchair once in the house. And then he went down the hill again and then up the hill again, helping his father to the other brown armchair in the house.

Finally, Billy closed the front door and flopped down exhausted on the sofa. His hands throbbed with the pain of pins and needles as the blood was once again allowed to flow through his aching fingers. His back screamed with the pain of bending over and carrying eight full bags of shopping. And with the pain of supporting his parents up the hill. His clothes stuck to him like a wet swimming costume as sweat poured down his face and body. Billy looked at his parents huffing and puffing in their comfy armchairs and said nothing. He had learnt this over many Saturdays over many years. Inside him, the unseen ball of hate for his parents just grew a bit bigger.

First, his father stared at Billy in disbelief.

Second, his mother stared at Billy in disbelief.

Then both of them stared at Billy in disbelief.

The huffing and puffing grew louder. But this was not because of horrible, physical exertion. Oh, no. This was a new kind of huffing and puffing of people who cannot believe their eyes. They cannot believe what they are seeing. And this also causes the onlooker to briefly lose the power of speech. How could this be? How could this boy, this child, who they had brought into the world, clothed and schooled and pampered – yes, pampered – with a Christmas toy, treat them like this? He was just sitting there on the sofa doing nothing. NOTHING! Can you believe it?

Mr Slurb was the first to regain the power of speech, 'Can you believe it, Mother? Our lazy child is just sat there while there is work to do.'

'No I can't, Father. I can't. How could he do this to us? Us, his own parents. There is work to do but he just sits there like a toad,' agreed Mrs Slurb.

'A wallowing pig.'

'A snoozing hippo.'

'And soon dinner will have to be made,' added Mr Slurb.

'Are we to starve because of this sloth?' added Mrs Slurb with alarm.

Billy said nothing. He dragged his weary body to the kitchen to do his next chore before dinner. Little did he realise that a terrible disaster was about to happen.

THE DISASTER

Billy put the last item of shopping, a tin of baked beans and sausages, on the shelf. It was a favourite night time snack of his mother who loved nothing better than sitting in bed snuffling the lot straight from the can.

'Is it all done?' asked Mrs Slurb from her comfy chair. She was busy stuffing her enormous face with a family sized pack of crisps. A fountain of soggy, chewed crisp bits flew from her mouth each time she spoke. 'Yes, it's about time, you idle leach.'

'Yes, me and your mother are starving. I can feel my ribs beginning to poke through,' added Mr Slurb feeling his bulbous flesh for bone.

Mrs Slurb heaved her bulk out of the chair and waddled her way to the kitchen. This was her heaven. She surveyed the tiled land for any signs of shopping. Nothing must get in the way of dinner. Nothing. Dinner was a sacred time in the Slurb household.

'Right. Pass me the chicken and be quick about it,' ordered Mrs Slurb the General.

Billy's heart skipped a beat. The colour drained from his face and his palms became sweaty and damp. He had not seen any chicken. He had not unpacked any chicken. What was he to do?

'Well, then. Where is it? Don't just stand there like a wet frog. Give me the chicken!'

Billy took a deep, frightened breath and stammered, 'There is no chicken.'

'WHAT?! NO CHICKEN?! Are you sure?' yelled Mrs Slurb in absolute shock.

'Yes...yes. We didn't buy one.'

Mrs Slurb had to steady herself by placing her chubby, great hand on the cooker. This was a disaster: no chicken! They ALWAYS had chicken on Saturday.

'Father, come quick,' squealed Mrs Slurb.

Responding to his wife's fearful voice, Mr Slurb slowly heaved his mammoth bulk out of the chair and waddled to the kitchen. Mr Slurb looked at Mrs Slurb's white face. He turned and looked at his son's trembling, pale face. And then he looked at his wife's white face again. Something was wrong.

'What's the matter? What's the little slug gone and done?' he asked, glaring at the boy.

'He says there is no chicken. That we didn't buy one,' Mrs Slurb spluttered out.

'WHAT?! NO CHICKEN?! But it's Saturday.' Quickly, like a bus reversing, Mr Slurb opened all the cupboard doors. No chicken. The fridge. NO chicken. The cooker. NO CHicken. Even the bin. NO CHICKEN! This was a disaster.

'I blame you,' Mr Slurb stated pointing a sausage-like finger at Billy.

'What can be done?' asked Mrs Slurb, glaring at Billy. 'Why didn't you remind us? I can't understand it. Do you want your family to starve? On a Saturday of all days?!'

'No,' said Billy in a tiny, trembling voice.

'There is only one thing to be done. You,' said Mr Slurb, stabbing his finger at Billy, 'You must go and buy a chicken.'

'Yes,' said Mrs Slurb, nodding in agreement, 'and if you don't find one, don't come back.'

'Quite right, mother. He should have reminded us. It is all his fault,' said Mr Slurb shoving some money into Billy's hands.

The decision made, the guilty judged, Mr Slurb and Mrs Slurb returned to their comfy armchairs. Billy stood in the kitchen trembling. He just had to get a chicken. Where could he get one? What could he do?

CHICKEN HUNT

Billy sped from the house as the dark clouds overhead let rip their torrent of rain. A chicken -- where to get a chicken? His feet thudded into the damp pavement as he turned the corner to the top of Wood Green high street. He was saved -- the Supermarket! Of course, why hadn't he thought of that? It *never* closes.

Billy strode happily towards the two great, glass doors of the Supermarket and pushed. Nothing. They didn't budge. They didn't open! No need to panic, he thought. In his eagerness, he must have pushed when he should have pulled. He tried again. Nothing. They didn't budge. SUPERMARKETS DON'T CLOSE! Billy frantically tried again and again, pushing and pulling, harder and harder. Nothing! They didn't budge! They didn't open - not even a millimetre! Billy pushed and pulled with all his strength in desperation.

'What do you think you're doing?' demanded a man dressed in a blue security uniform who seemed to have appeared out of nowhere next to Billy.

Billy slowly dragged his eyes away from the doors to the man with the slightly-too-long, grey moustache.

'I...I'm trying to get in. I need a chicken,' Billy stammered.

'Well, it's shut. The door's shut,' the man stated unhelpfully.

'But Supermarkets don't shut,' Billy pleaded.

'This one has. Problem with the tills – gremlin in the works,' he explained.

Billy began to walk slowly away to continue his quest.

'Good luck with your chicken hunt,' called the man.

Billy took a quick glance back just as the man seemed to disappear in the shadows with an odd twinkle in his eyes. Billy continued to jog along the high street, his sodden feet squelching like great sponges on the pavestones as his eyes darted this way and that for an open shop likely to sell chicken. He knew it would be an evening of nagging misery as he waited for the following day if he didn't find a chicken. His parents would have him doing twice as much as usual to correct his unforgivable failure:

'Clean the guttering, you worm.'
'Scrub the toilet you, slug.'
'Brats like you need to learn...'
'Not to treat your parents' like mugs.'
'Cut the grass, you toad.'
'Mop the floor, you maggot.'
'This will stop such behaviour...'
'From becoming a bad habit.'

An almost endless list of chores that would leave him exhausted and sore with no time to play. Not that he had friends to play with. Who wanted to be friends with a Slurb?

Billy ran with renewed hope towards a store whose neon lights lit it up like a great, welcoming Christmas Tree only to notice too late a small card in the window:

SHOP CLOSED - Cats Out of the Bag Over Our Fish.

With that, Billy plodded sadly on his way. Each step of his feet seemed to say: Got to get a chicken; Got to get a chicken; Or your life won't be worth living; Got to get a chicken; To save your day. But again and again, all he found was closed store after closed store with notices on their doors or windows. ALL the shops in Wood Green seemed closed. The rain lashed down harder, stinging his face, as he reached the bottom of the high street, where he stopped next to a shop with yet another sign on its door:

SORRY CLOSED - ILLNESS. Frog in the Throat.

There were no more shops left to try. He had failed. Great sadness welled up from deep down somewhere in his stomach to form tears behind his eyes.

'What's up, son?' asked a man with a kindly face, dressed in a blue shirt.

Billy looked at him, startled. He had not noticed the man there with the slightly-too-long, grey beard. Billy could say nothing. What could he say? How could he explain to this stranger why a chicken was so important? It would seem foolish. There was nothing that could be done. No one could help.

'You better get home, son. You're soaking wet,' the man suggested kindly.

'Thanks,' Billy quietly muttered and turned slowly away. His eyes blinked in the pouring rain into which the man seemed to disappear. Billy breathed out one big, deep, sad sigh and made his way towards home with the empty shopping bag dripping in his hand.

THE SHOP ON THE CORNER

Billy rounded the corner of Ringwald Road, his heart as weighted as his footsteps. Through the drizzling grey of rain, he peered up towards his house and let out another deep sigh. He was just about to take the last few steps to it when he noticed, out of the corner of his eye, a dim light. A dim light of a shop! That was odd, he thought. He had never noticed that shop there before. But then, he spent his days looking at his feet, weighted down by shopping or any other items his parents wanted carried. Would it be open? It was worth a try.

Billy crossed over to the shop and his heart sank as he spied a sign on the door, CLOSED. He laughed bitterly and was about to turn away when an unseen hand changed it to OPEN. What a stroke of luck! Billy tried to take a quick peek through one of the old windows but much of the glass was covered with faded, black and white advertisements and the rest was covered with dirty smears making it impossible to see inside. Oh well, he thought. What did he have to lose? And with that, he pushed against the stiff door.

The shop door swung open suddenly, sending Billy inside so quickly that he almost tripped over the small man crouched on the other side.

'Sorry,' Billy spluttered with embarrassment.

'The man looked up quickly, smiled, and went back to what he was doing. He was banging extraordinarily long nails into an extraordinarily worn rug to fix it to the wooden floor.

'Please excuse,' the small man said. 'This thing has a habit of lifting up and catching people's feet. Most bothersome.'

Billy skirted carefully around the man and searched for any sign that this might be the sort of shop that sold chickens. It was very unlike any corner shop he had been in before but it was one. It appeared covered from floor to ceiling with wooden shelves crammed with boxes, tins and jars of every shape. Each jar contained items of different colours: some watery, some swirling mists. To make up for the lack of free shelf space, the owner had decided to make use of the ceiling so that there was an assortment of pans, jars, saucepans, wheels and other oddments hanging from different lengths of string from the ceiling.

'Yes?' said a voice from behind, what looked like, piles of old newspapers. 'What are you after?'

'Er...Do you sell chickens?' Billy asked doubtfully.

'Yes, of course we do. We have one left, right at the back of the shop,' said the voice.

'Thank you!' Billy exclaimed joyfully and began to head quickly in that direction.

'WAIT! You'll need this,' said the voice as it sent the piles of paper crashing to the floor. The owner of the voice was wearing a long, baggy, light-blue shirt with a particularly high collar and particularly long sleeves.

'Here,' said the shopkeeper, holding out a candlestick holder with a candle that he lit with a long match. 'It's dark down there and the lights don't always work too well, if at all,' he explained as his slightly-too-long grey moustache and beard shimmered in the candle's light.

'Er, thanks,' said Billy, taking the candle carefully and heading towards the back of the shop.

The journey to the back seemed to take longer than he thought it would. And each step seemed to take him past shelves with stranger and stranger items: dusty glass balls containing swirling colours; dried leathery scales in a jar; a twig broom chained to a great anchor; rusty armour hanging from the beams. The place seemed enormous. Finally, Billy reached the small, white, metal fridge at the back. The lid was stiff so he had to place the candle on the floor. Please let it be there, thought Billy as he forced open the lid. Inside Billy found a chicken. Just a chicken and nothing more. He put it carefully inside his wet shopping bag, picked up the candle, and made his way to the front of the shop to pay.

'Ah, you found it,' said the shopkeeper in the overlong shirt.

'Yes,' said Billy.

'Good. Now the price – it's quite costly I'm afraid,' said the man as the light of the candle made his eyes dance.

'Oh,' said Billy expecting the worse.

'Two pounds and a promise.'

Had Billy heard him right? A promise?

'That's right, a promise. Don't worry, it's nothing bad,' said the shopkeeper with a kindly smile. 'Just promise to make a wish with the chicken's wishbone.'

'Oh, I will,' Billy eagerly agreed. He then quickly paid the money, hopped around the small man still hammering nails into the old rug, and sped home.

THE WISHBONE

'Where have you been, you leech?' was the pleasant welcome Mrs Slurb gave Billy as he squelched into the house.

'Buying a chicken,' Billy stated.

'Don't you get all smart-mouthed with your mother. What took you so long, you squid?' Mr Slurb demanded from his throne of an armchair.

Billy sighed and explained quickly what had happened. He was cold, wet and wanted to change. His parents had not noticed. His parents never noticed. It was not that they were being *deliberately* unkind and mean. It was like they were children in grown-up bodies. BIG selfish children. Big children that did not share. Big children that never thought of others. It's not *really* their fault. They don't know better. Perhaps they were spoilt when they *were* young. Or perhaps they did not have parents who loved them or did not have many toys. Mr and Mrs

Slurb were *these children* in grown-up bodies.

'Hmmm. Ok, then,' said Mr Slurb, happy at having heard all he wanted to hear. 'Now, stop your chatter. I'm missing UGLY CHEF.'

Mrs Slurb looked down at her dripping son and snatched the bag from his hand like it was precious treasure.

'You're making the carpet wet. I don't want to have to clean it,' which she **never** did. 'Get changed.'

And with that, Billy was free until dinner. He sped like a bullet to his room.

Downstairs in the kitchen, Mrs Slurb ruled. It was her kingdom and the **ONLY** place she did *anything* in the house. The chicken was roasting to a lovely golden colour in the oven. Occasionally, she would turn on the oven light and check on its progress. *Is it ready yet? Is it ready yet?* Her whole body was saying this as great drips of drool formed on her lips. She impatiently returned to her kitchen stool, heaving her huge bottom onto its groaning surface and carried on watching her favourite SOAP on the kitchen television. The wait was almost unbearable. Chicken was her favourite.

Suddenly, a loud **RING** sounded from the oven and Mrs Slurb knew it was at last ready and time for action. She waddled swiftly over to the row of three microwave machines. Quickly, she tore open FATIMA'S SPEEDY-COOK ROAST POTATOES and put them in the first microwave. Next, she ripped open FATIMA'S SPEEDY-COOK VEGETABLES IN LARD and placed those in the second microwave. Finally, wiping the sweat from her brow, she opened FATIMA'S EXTRA-THICK GRAVY and popped that in the last microwave. She quickly set the microwaves to one minute, pressed start and removed the glorious chicken from the oven. She proudly took it through to the dining table as a three-PING salute sounded from the microwaves: dinner was ready!

Billy looked at his parents across the dinner table. Or, at least, he tried. As usual, Mr Slurb was hidden behind a great mountain of chicken, a hill of roast potatoes and three vegetables in an ocean of gravy. As usual, Mrs Slurb was hidden behind an enormous mountain of chicken, a hill of roast potatoes and one vegetable in a lake of gravy. Billy then looked down at his two thin slices of chicken, three potatoes and a mound of vegetables in a teaspoon of gravy. He began to eat. As usual, the potatoes tasted rubbery and could easily been used as footballs. As usual, the vegetables were soggy and could have easily been used as flannels. He sighed. At least the chicken would taste all right. And he cut himself a small piece and placed it on his tongue. Maybe it was because he was very tired. Maybe it was because he still felt damp, wet and miserable to his bones. He did not know. But the chicken tasted *quite* good. In fact, it tasted *so* quite good, he began to feel a bit dizzy and laugh to himself. He glanced at his parents and a funny idea popped into his head. A ridiculous idea: he wanted to pull the wishbone. He wanted to make a wish. Yes, of course those wishes *never* come true. Of course, it *never* was going to work. But still...

'Dad,' Billy said, fighting to contain the dizzy laughter growing inside.

Mr Slurb almost spluttered cannonballs of potato over his wife. His son never interrupted dinner with foolish chatter. He knew how important meal times were.

'Dad,' Billy repeated. There was no stopping him now. He was struggling to keep the dizzy laughter in his throat. 'Can we pull the chicken's wishbone?'

'Hmmm,' Mr Slurb stated, quite shocked at the second interruption. 'Ok. Then will you let me eat in peace?' he wearily asked as gravy dribbled like a stream down his chin.

'Yes. I promise.'

Mrs Slurb watched in amazement as Mr Slurb stopped eating while there was food on his plate. He then put down his fork, pulled the wishbone from the few remains of the chicken on the table and offered part of the bone to the boy. Billy reached across the table and hooked his little finger around one end of the greasy bone.

Billy looked at his father whose mouth crashed through boulders of potato as gravy oozed over his gums.

Billy looked at his mother whose jaws churned over chunks of chicken as fat dribbled down her neck.

The ball of hate inside him burst.

He knew what he would wish for. And with that, he pulled hard on the bone. There was a small snap. Billy stared down at the piece of bone in his hooked finger. It was bigger. He had won. He got to make the wish. Without a moment's thought, he made a silent wish in his head: *I wish* I had different parents. *I wish* I had parents that got out of their chairs, moved, did sport.

'No more stopping me eating with your foolishness,' glared Mr Slurb.

As he climbed tiredly into his shabby bed, Billy had to laugh at himself. What a silly, odd thing he had done at dinner. And how strange that his father had stopped eating for long enough to pull the bone. Stranger still, that he had not really lost his temper. It had been a most unusual Saturday. Billy smiled down at the piece of wishbone that he held in his hand. It was just a chicken bone. Nothing special. Wishes do not really come true. Sighing, he placed it on the small table by his head and went to sleep. The bone sat there unmoving, seeming to almost shimmer and sparkle in the moonlight.

SOMETHING NEW

That night, Billy had strange dreams of dimly lit shops with giggling brooms and laughing fridges forming a strange circle. In the centre of them all were supermarket chickens: some small, some tall, some blue, some green -- a complete range of all the colours and sizes you could imagine. All of them were dancing and swirling, this way and that, in an odd, headless ball while singing a joyful clucking song.

'Wakey, wakey!'

It took a moment for Billy to understand this voice was not part of the dream. He opened his tired blurry eyes to find the room in pale darkness. *What was going on?* His parents **NEVER** got up before daylight. NOT UNTIL he had served them breakfast in bed. What had he done *so* wrong? Billy rubbed his eyes to try to bring everything into focus.

A white tracksuit.

A WHITE TRACKSUIT! Billy sat bolt upright, his jaw gaping open at the shock of what he saw. There, stood at the end of the bed, was Mr Slurb. At least, it looked a bit like Mr Slurb. This one was wearing a gleaming-white tracksuit, was slim, muscular and was JOGGING ON THE SPOT! Billy was speechless.

Another shock was just around the corner. In came Mrs Slurb. At least it looked something like Mrs Slurb. This one was wearing a perfect, pale-blue tracksuit, was slim, muscular and was JOGGING!

'Get up lazy bones,' Mrs Slurb said cheerfully, tossing a tracksuit and trainers on the bed. 'We want to get a move on.'

'Come on, come on,' added Mr Slurb impatiently whilst doing a couple of *energetic* squat thrusts. 'We'll miss our little morning run.'

Billy wearily crawled out of bed as his parents back-flipped out of the bedroom. His hands shook as he put on the clothes. *What had happened?* It wasn't the outfits that had so shaken Billy. Or the exercises that they had been doing. Or even, the fact, Mr and Mrs Slurb looked somewhat different, in a thinner way. Oh no. The *most* shocking thing, the *most* terrifying thing that made him shiver inside and the hairs stand up on the back of his neck was that his parents were SMILING at him. Can you imagine such a strange thing? Billy's parents **never** smiled at him. Not even on his birthday.

Billy yawned loudly and stretched his arms. He slowly tied his shoelaces and glanced at the bedside clock. Five o'clock! It was five o'clock on a Sunday morning! What were these new parents thinking, going running at this time? What was wrong with them? It was then Billy noticed the wishbone piece on the small table next to the clock, glistening in the dim light. He remembered. Billy picked up the bone and peered at it intently. It still seemed to be just a chicken bone but Billy now knew differently. Hidden inside there was

something special. Magical, maybe. He
carefully put the bone in his trouser pocket,
zipped it carefully up and hurried down
stairs.

Billy sat down for breakfast with Mr and
Mrs Slurb. He felt extremely hungry after
last night's strange events. **What a
difference.** He got to sit down instead of
having to cook fourteen sausages, four fried
eggs and twelve pieces of fried bread for
his old parents. These *new* parents were
fabulous! He was actually sitting down with
them and he was going to **eat!**
Smiling, Billy looked eagerly down into his
breakfast bowl. The smile disappeared. He
peered closely at the brown chunks within.
They looked like cardboard. He gingerly
prodded one. They felt like cardboard. He
nibbled one on its corner. It tasted like
cardboard.
'What's this?' asked Billy.
'Your breakfast, of course,' stated Mrs
Slurb cheerily. 'ULTRA BRAN CHUNKS.'

'Oh.'

'Now, pour on some milk. We need to get a move on,' added Mr Slurb.

Billy poured on some milk. It was not normal milk. It was not lovely, cool white milk. Instead, it was a grey-brown colour. It looked like stewed paper. It tasted like stewed paper.

'What's this milk?' asked Billy, slowly crunching his way through one spoonful of the cardboard tasting cereal with stewed-paper milk.

'Soya milk, of course,' stated Mrs Slurb cheerily as she finished her bowl of breakfast.

'Chop, chop,' said Mr Slurb leaping up from the table to perform a few warm-up stretches. 'Winners don't delay.'

'I'm not hungry,' Billy said putting down his spoon and leaving the bowl of revolting stuff.

'Can't wait to get started, hey? That's my boy,' said Mr Slurb slapping Billy heartily on the back. 'Let's get moving then!'

THE FUN RUN

Five seconds later, Billy caught up with both parents at the smartly-painted front door. Mrs Slurb stood fidgeting and glancing at her watch. Mr Slurb stood impatiently tapping his foot beside a large backpack.

'Finally,' said Mr Slurb, 'I thought you'd never get here.'

Billy glanced at both parents. There was something not quite right. There was something **very** odd. That was it! Both were wearing full backpacks! Mr and Mrs Slurb *never* carried *anything.* Billy *always* carried *everything.*

'Here's your backpack,' said Mr Slurb, grabbing the large backpack off the floor and throwing it at Billy, almost sending him through the nearby wall.

Billy heaved up the item on to his back which immediately complained. It weighed like a bag of elephants sat on a mountain. What could be in all these packs? Perhaps some sort of delicious picnic for after the run?

There is running and then there is the *Slurb's little morning run*. You may think those who run in a marathon have a tough time of it, particularly those strange people who decide to make the trek a little more jolly by wearing thick, furry costumes in the blazing sun. Or you may feel sorry for that Greek soldier who had to run one hundred and fifty miles across hot country just to deliver a little message. But these are **nothing** compared to the *Slurb's little morning run*.

It began easily enough, a pleasant jog up his road's gentle slope of a hill with the straps of the backpack lightly jarring into Billy's collarbones with each step. Then quick turn to the left, down the narrow alleyway, tripping in potholes, crashing through stabbing nettles and skidding in fresh dog poo. Each poo bigger than the previous one. Billy didn't know what the owners had been feeding their dogs but he

had a strong suspicion it was ULTRA BRAN
CHUNKS.

'Enough of the gentle warm-up. Now let's
really get going!' said Mr Slurb, propelling
Billy forward with a hearty slap on the back
before he set off like a rocket.

Then it was over a green, pass some railings
and down some steps. Mr Slurb bounding
down. Mrs Slurb jumping down. Billy tripping
down. Squelching and squerching along a
boggy path, showering mud-drops. Mud-
drops squirming in his ears, splattering in his
eyes, sliding down his mouth. The worse kind
of mud. Stinky, lumpy, black-soup mud made
from stagnant water like six-day-old toilet
paper mixed with unwashed socks. Then it
was along the riverbank, splashing in mud
puddles, being bitten by gnats. The pack was
stabbing at his bones. *This was worse than
shopping!*

Thankfully, Mr and Mrs Slurb had stopped
up ahead in a surprisingly mudless spot made
up of clumps of grass and large, flat stones.
But this was not the most surprising thing

that Billy saw as he splashed through yet another black-soup puddle and stopped in front of both of them. He rubbed his eyes to check. How could it be? Mr Slurb stood waiting in his still pristine white tracksuit and Mrs Slurb stood waiting in her still pristine pale-blue tracksuit. The muddy shower had not touched Mr Slurb! It had not even dropped on Mrs Slurb! They had no gnats and didn't smell of dog poo. Apparently, the alleyway had not had anything against them, neither had the puddles. Fed up and aching, Billy hoped this was where they were going to stop and have the picnic.

'Isn't this great fun? Can you imagine anything better?' said Mr Slurb full of good cheer and enthusiasm.

Billy could imagine *anything* better that this run: lying in bed, watching TV or even *tidying his room.* But he said nothing. After all, this Mr and Mrs Slurb were friendly towards him and seemed to like him. They didn't yell at him or call him names. This *had* to be better than life before.

'It's great,' Billy lied.

'Enough chatter you two. Let's get moving,' Mrs Slurb tut-tutted playfully and then led the way across the river using a line of stepping stones with Mr Slurb in hot pursuit. Reaching the other riverbank, they sped up the slope and into a field of tall grass.

Billy slipped and skidded on the stones, fell in the river, got out, fell in, covering himself in half-chewed fish, got out, fell in, covering himself in river weed, got out, clambered up the slope and staggered blindly into the field of grass.

Billy's back cried in pain that the extra weight of the water had added to the pack so that it was as heavy as a bag of elephants sat on a mountain while holding gorillas. But that was not the worst thing! Billy now smelt of dog poo, splattered stagnant mud, river weed and half-chewed fish. Of course, this is absolutely delicious to gnats so they now had guests over for a bite to eat. But worse still was Billy couldn't see his parents. He blindly ran forward, following a trail of flattened grass and swishing noises, darting this way and that as it changed direction, brushing gnats and grass from his eyes, stumbling on hidden stones, cutting his knees. Then he met a cow.

Now, there are many ways to greet a cow in a field. The one *not* to use at *any time* is to run full pelt into its bottom. The cow, called Hilda, was most annoyed at this unpleasant greeting. She glared at the boy and mooed angrily. **MOOOAM!**

Billy ran. The cow came roaring after him, flattening grass. Billy felt its hot breath on his neck. His back and neck screaming in pain, feet stumbling, running over the earth. **MOOOAM!** came the deafening roar in his ear. Blindly he ran, hoping he would soon reach the field's edge and escape. **MOOOAM!** Was that a cow's nose he could feel? **MOOAM!** Blindly he ran, straight into a fence, half climbing, half falling over. The cow glared at him, snorting in disgust.

'Ah, there you are,' said Mrs Slurb, calling from further down by the fence. 'We wondered where you got to and I see you made a friend.'

'I'm afraid you'll have to leave it behind as the park is just over this rise,' added Mr Slurb, setting off in the direction shown by a precise nod of his head.

Groaning, Billy heaved himself up from the ground, with the insects happily hovering around him, and trailed after his parents. Was any picnic worth all this?

When Billy staggered into the park, almost dragging his weary body across the grass, he found Mr Slurb doing one-armed press-ups while Mrs Slurb was doing the splits, much to the shock and amazement of passers-by. It was then he noticed something that almost brought tears of joy to his eyes: his parents had taken off their rucksacks! At last, it was time to rest and eat. Billy peeled his heavy load from his sweaty, muddy, slimy back and dropped it to the ground along with himself.

A PICNIC IN THE PARK

Billy eagerly unzipped his backpack and felt something hard and tube shaped inside. Odd, he thought. Perhaps it was a flask of drink?

'Can't wait to get started, hey?' commented Mr Slurb.

'That's our boy,' said Mrs Slurb looking on proudly.

Billy pulled out a large, weighty barbell. He had to blink twice to check he was not seeing things. No. It was a barbell. Perhaps the food was underneath? He stuck his hand into the pack again and to his horror discovered another hard, tube shaped object. Another barbell. In desperate hunger, he tipped the bag up, emptying its contents on the ground: dumbbells, a chest expander, hand grips and ankle weights. And nothing else. Maybe his parents had the food.

Mesmerised, Billy stared as Mr and Mrs Slurb unzipped their packs and emptied them. Out came two shots, a medicine ball, a hammer, stop watches, kettlebells and the latest issue of PAIN AND FITNESS magazine. No picnic. No food. Not even a health food bar. Not a crumb. Billy couldn't help but let out a small groan.

'Sorry, Billy. We know you can't wait to get started. We'll be ready soon enough,' consoled Mrs Slurb as she smiled at her sad little star.

What followed can only be described as physical torture and Mr and Mrs Slurb seemed to revel in it. There was not a part of his body that Billy didn't stretch, twist or bend. Not even an eyelash. Then there were the weights!

Billy entered his home exhausted. The gnats and their friends bid a sad farewell to their favourite dish as he staggered to the sofa, sunk down and fell instantly to sleep. Not even the pungent perfume of poo, weed and fish was powerful enough to wake him. Mr Slurb looked proudly down at his protégée, his tracksuit gleaming in the light, and began some lunges and press-ups to pass the time. Mrs Slurb made her way to the kitchen to prepare lunch.

LUNCH

A tired, aching and bruised Billy made his way to the glass topped dining table and he perched himself on the violent green, moulded plastic seats. The recent shower had failed to make any of his aches and pains feel any better. His stomach rumbled a drumroll as Mrs Slurb entered from the kitchen.

Mr Slurb began to tuck in eagerly, swallowing great gulps. Mrs Slurb took hers more slowly, preferring to savour each delightful flavour. Billy just looked down at his, puzzled. There was no plate, no bowl, just a jug. A jug like one of those you might see in a scientist's lab, Dr Frankenstein's. It did not contain *anything* Billy could recognise as food. Instead, it contained a gloopy, green mixture that bubbled, burped and farted at him. It was a swamp.

'Anything wrong?' asked Mrs Slurb concerned at Billy's lack of appetite.

'Er...what is it?'

'You know, our favourite. Brussels, cabbage and spinach mixed with raw egg and soya yoghurt,' she replied sipping at hers. 'Green Smoothie, of course.'

'Oh,' said Billy peering at it suspiciously.

'Eat up,' commanded Mr Slurb. 'You need to keep your strength up for the rest of the day.'

Mr and Mrs Slurb watched Billy intently, broad smiles across their faces, drinking from their blurping jugs.

Under such pressure, there was only one thing Billy could do. He took in a deep breath, tried to tell his nose to close, and swallowed a mouthful. Down it slowly slid like cold, matted custard with lumps. He could feel those cold lumps of mashed cabbage, spinach and Brussels coated in slimy egg and soya yoghurt crawl up over his teeth, fall onto his tongue and then squirm down his throat.

Billy leapt up from his chair, ran past the astonished parents, grabbed a bowl from the kitchen and sped up the stairs. He was sick. Violently sick.

'Oh no,' said Mr Slurb deeply concerned.

'I'll go check on him,' said Mrs Slurb.

In the bathroom, Billy was sat on the toilet with the bowl on his lap, green swampy liquid shooting out of his nose, mouth and bottom. Billy began to suspect he had made a mistake when he wished for new parents.

Mrs Slurb entered the room, sighing deeply, and lightly kissed Billy on the head.

'Oh, I do hope you're not falling ill,' she said looking at him full of concern. 'Everyone will be so disappointed if you miss your match.'

Billy groaned as a shower of glorious green splashed into the bowl.

THE MATCH

Billy trotted excitedly along the corridor towards the dressing room. He was feeling a lot better now and was no longer hungry. He had managed to persuade Mr and Mrs Slurb that the best thing for him would be a helping of fish and chips followed by ice-cream. He had eagerly devoured the food leaving the plate sparkling white. Mrs Slurb had been disappointed that he had not finished his delicious *Green Smoothie* but would have been more saddened if Billy had missed his match. So, all in all, she was glad he seemed on the mend and had his appetite back. It must have been a bug, she decided.

'This is going to be brilliant!' said Mr Slurb who was almost popping with excitement. 'I can't wait to see the look on the other lot's faces when you win. I've been looking forward to this for ages!'

Billy looked up at Mr Slurb nervously. He was usually the boy who got picked last for the football teams at school although he

49

loved playing. Perhaps things here would be different now he had used the wishbone.

Mr Slurb gently pushed Mrs Slurb and Billy in the back, urging them forwards towards the dressing room.

'Now then, father. We don't want Billy to suffer any silly accidents due to your impatience. It will all start soon enough,' cautioned Mrs Slurb with a wink.

Billy was ushered into the dressing room by his increasingly excitable parents. There he was greeted by four white walls, a single wooden bench and a locker. There were no other football players changing. There were no football kits hanging up. There was no one else. At first, this struck Billy as being odd but then he realised it must be because he was late. That was why Mr Slurb had been in such a hurry to get there.

'Hurry up and get dressed. You don't want to keep everyone waiting,' said Mrs Slurb. 'I'm off to find myself a good seat,' and she left the room.

Billy opened the holdall Mr Slurb had handed him and quickly pulled on an oversized pair of shiny, red shorts followed by red socks. No football shirt.

'I have no shirt!' Billy exclaimed.

'Why do you need a shirt for?' said Mr Slurb, quite puzzled. 'No one wears a shirt. The match is indoors.'

Billy wondered at this strange statement. A football match with **no** shirts? He hadn't heard of football players not wearing shirts *until* after they scored a goal. Or at the end of a match. Maybe there was something wrong with the heating?

Billy put on the boots and looked up. He saw Mr Slurb holding something that made him tremble inside and his heart leap into his mouth. They were big. They were red. They were boxing gloves. BOXING GLOVES! His whole body seemed to scream in panic.

'Here you are son. Bet you can't wait to get out there and get stuck in and do some serious damage!' said Mr Slurb enthusiastically as he carefully tied on the enormous gloves.   Billy's whole mind seemed to float and leave his body. He didn't want to be there. He hardly noticed as Mr Slurb tied a red, padded protector on his head.

In a daze, Billy was led from the changing room, down a brightly lit corridor, to the main hall. Sheep-like, he was pulled up to the stage.

'In the left corner, a local lad from London, we have *Bullseye Billy* and in the right corner, all the way from Wales, we have *Smasher Steffan.*'

Billy's heart pounded in his chest almost drowning out the screams and cries from the audience. Mr Slurb's last-minute encouraging words in his ear went straight inside and out the other. Was he really here? Was this really happening to him?

The sounding of the bell brought Billy out of his daze and unsteadily he stood facing his opponent. Steffan cast a big shadow over the quaking Billy. Steffan was big. VERY big. UNUSUALLY BIG. His arms were as thick as truck tyres and his head as large as a boulder.

'Bash him, Billy!' screamed Mrs Slurb from her front row seat, sending her popcorn over everyone.

Billy gulped.

As the first great hammer-fisted blow hit the side of his head, Billy realised he had made a mistake.

That night, as he clambered into bed, his face bruised, his bones sore, his soul tired, Billy regretted his decision. He peered down at the small, dull, chicken bone fragment sat on the table by his bed. Perhaps things were best when you left them as they were. Perhaps that was his mistake. Sadly, with puffed-purple eyes, Billy grasped the wishbone. Maybe. Just maybe, he was allowed one more wish. Clinging tightly to the piece of bone, his fingers clasping desperately around its fragile form, Billy wished to return to home, to the Slurbs, to the ones he knew.

BREAKFAST

That night, Billy had bizarre dreams of stretching boxing gloves and back-flipping backpacks forming a strange, circular ring around a roped stage. On the stage were supermarket chickens dressed in shiny outfits: some small, some tall, some black, some blue – a complete array of all the disgusting colours and sizes you could imagine. All of them were dodging and weaving, this way and that, trying to land a blow on each other with their plucked, scrawny wings whilst being cheered on by a braying crowd.

'Oi! Get up you lazy tapeworm! We want our breakfast!'

Billy opened his eyes to see a huge form he instantly recognised. That bulbous, hairy belly hanging over crumpled pyjama bottoms below a jam-stained top could *only* belong to *his* Mr Slurb.

'I said get up you lazy slug. We're starving and waiting for breakfast!' yelled Mr Slurb, kicking the bed. He immediately broke into a sweat because of the effort involved. Glaring at Billy, Mr Slurb then turned and left the room; scratching his elephantile bottom.

Billy shot out of bed, got dressed and made his way down stairs. That's odd. He felt no aches or pains, no twinges nor spasms *at all.* He rubbed a circular patch of dust off from the hallway mirror and peered at the cracked reflection of himself. No bruising. No cuts. **Not a scratch.** It was as if none of it had ever happened. Perhaps it had all been a horrible, painfully vivid nightmare.

'Hurry up with that food, you useless leech! I'm starting to look like a skeleton,' screeched Mrs Slurb from her bed.

Billy sped into the kitchen to make breakfast before he got himself into any more trouble. He flung open the cupboard door, grabbed four large frying pans and placed them on the hob. He quickly yanked open the cupboard and grabbed the lard.

Using a large spoon, Billy scooped and dolloped a lump of lard in the middle of each pan and turned on the heat.

In one frying pan went *twelve* slices of fatty bacon rashers that sizzled and spat in protest. In the second, he broke *eight* large eggs that glooped and spread into each other. In the next went *six* large pork sausages that rolled happily about in the fat. In the final frying pan leapt four pieces of white bread that tanned themselves slowly. Billy went from pan to pan with a fish slice, checking the progress of the food, trying to avoid the spits of fat and hisses of steam.

After what seemed an eternity, the food was ready. Billy arranged four plates in a row. On the first went the bacon, followed by the eggs on the next, then the sausages on the third and the fried bread on the last plate. Billy grabbed a tray, carefully balanced the plates on it and was about to set off when he remembered the tea. He had forgotten the tea!

Flicking on the kettle, Billy put two tea bags into the brown teapot with some milk and *fifteen* sugars. (His parents hated the strain of having to pour the milk into the tea cup).

Finally! The kettle had boiled. Billy splashed the water into the pot, put the lid on, balanced the pot on the crowded tray, heaved it up and made his way upstairs.

Mr and Mrs Slurb sat in their bed eagerly awaiting breakfast. The TV was on by their feet showing one of Mrs Slurb's favourite reality shows. Billy staggered into the room, carrying the heavy tray to the bed. Mr Slurb snatched it from him, placed it on his lap and said, 'You forgot the brown sauce.'

'Sorry,' mumbled Billy and turned to leave.

'And don't take too long making your mother's breakfast, either,' added Mr Slurb, taking a long slurp of tea from his teapot.

THINGS CHANGE

The weeks began to pass by for Billy and he got used to the usual routine of insults, chores, school, chores, Saturday chicken and feeling exhausted. A new, unseen ball of hate began to grow inside, each day a little more darkness added to it by his parents' selfish, uncaring behaviour. Yet in the sock drawer, in his bedroom, the wishbone piece remained, almost forgotten, a distant symbol of shattered hopes and impossible dreams.

Although Billy wasn't happy, it was an unhappiness he was used to like a slight burn. He could feel it. He knew it was there but he was used to the sensation. Besides, Billy felt it was safer to leave the bone alone after what seemed to happen to him last time he messed with things. It was a dangerous thing, a wish. At least with *these* parents he knew what to expect.

Then things changed.

Billy trudged up the hill after school. Like most children his age, Billy didn't particularly enjoy school and all the work he had to do. Yet, at least at school he was free. At school, he didn't have to jump to his parents' demands and listen to the insults thrown his way. Ok, he didn't really have any friends and thought himself lucky to be included in the odd football match but at least it was a moment of freedom. And each of these moments were precious.

Billy braced himself for what waited for him at home as he neared the front door. Maybe he could just sneak in and up to his room for a little while. Just half an hour of freedom before facing the parents.

Turning his key in the lock, Billy silently pushed open the door. No sound of them. He clicked the door quietly shut, removed his shoes without a sound and began to tip-toe towards the stairs. He didn't dare breathe.

'Oi! Get here, you!' commanded Mr Slurb from the front room.

Sighing, Billy dumped his bag in the hall and dragged himself in to find Mr Slurb sat in his armchair, dunking a black pudding into a mug of gravy and biting off huge chunks. Mrs Slurb was happily munching on a bread and dripping sandwich.

Taking a moment to bang on his chest to help a rather large lump of sausage go down, Mr Slurb told Billy, 'Your mother and me have got a dog. All our friends have one so we got one and it will be good for company. Besides, it will help protect the house and take care of all the scraps left over from meals.'

This amazed Billy. There were **NEVER** any scraps left over. His parents would eat the plates if they could. The poor dog would starve.

'So, this is Cuddles,' stated Mrs Slurb as she tore off a piece of her sandwich and gave it to the unseen animal behind a corner of her chair.

This was shocking! He just couldn't believe it! His mother was sharing her food!

Billy approached Mrs Slurb's chair slowly, not wanting to frighten the creature with any sudden loud sounds or movements. Perhaps Cuddles and Billy could be friends. He could have someone to play with and snuggle up to. A friend that would make his life bearable.

Peering around the corner of the armchair, Billy could just make out its thick, round skull and chocolate-brown fur as Mrs Slurb caressed its short ears. He held out his hand, took another small step forward, and went to stroke Cuddle's head. Immediately, the dog sat up and glaring at Billy, let out a skin-stripping snarl. Billy froze, unable to take his eyes off the beast's powerful, crushing jaws. His heart seemed to pound like a kettle drum in his chest.

'Aww. Don't you upset, Cuddles. She was nice and comfy lying on the floor,' said Mrs Slurb, rubbing the poor dog's ears consolingly.

'Yeh. Don't you upset her. She's delicate, you know. She needs proper looking after. She's a pedigree, after all, unlike you,' said

Mr Slurb, taking a meaningful bite of black pudding.

Billy backed slowly away from the snarling beast towards the door. Maybe it just needed time to get used to him.

'Where you going?' asked Mr Slurb.

'To my bedroom,' said Billy, shooting a quick glance at his escape route.

'Oh no you don't. Have you forgotten the washing-up?' said Mr Slurb as he slurped on some gravy.

'And you need to get Cuddles her din-dins,' added Mrs Slurb, eyeing the dog fondly. 'Isn't that right, Cuddles? Who needs her din-dins, then?'

'Yeh, that's right. Besides your other few jobs, you have to feed, walk and clean up after Cuddles. Get going,' commanded Mr Slurb as he jabbed a greasy, gravy-dripping black pudding towards the kitchen.

Cautiously, Billy backed out of the room into the kitchen. It was dreadful. He would have *even more* jobs to do but maybe, just maybe, it would be worth it. And holding on to that thought, Billy began to tackle the great mountain of washing-up.

THE DOG

Billy got up at six to start his chores. After dressing, he took a few deep breaths of air in the hallway then tied a scarf around his lower face. Next, he picked up the trowel and a plastic bag from the cupboard under the stairs. He entered the kitchen and quietly turned the key in the back door. This was the moment. Billy opened the door a crack to check the coast was clear, then stepped into the back garden. He did this every day.

The garden was poorly named. It was just a mass of churned up mud and forlorn grass. Nothing could grow there. Cuddles saw to that. Any plant young and foolish enough to show its head above the soil was soon torn to shreds by the beast. All that remained was a chewed stump where once an apple tree had been.

Billy looked towards the back of the garden where the dog kennel stood. In front of it was an enormous bone, as big as a child's leg. It was Cuddle's midnight snack, just in case she got peckish in the night. Cuddles lay in her kennel, one eye open, not moving as long as there was food in front of her, or nearby or she was about to be fed. Occasionally, she would let out a low, rumbling growl just to let Billy know she was there. She could wait for him. She was a patient dog.

Billy sighed, tightened the scarf around his face and looked down at the most prominent feature of the garden: the patchwork of light and dark that lay like a splattering of brown chocolate on top of the mud. This was the thing you could not escape with every step and breath. This was why he was there.

Billy just could not believe that one, single animal could produce so much poo in one day. Nowhere was safe. There was not a grain of soil that had escaped. Billy bent down and began the enormous task of scooping up each individual pile and slopping it into the plastic bag (at least **now** he had a trowel). Each scoop caused him to gag, cough and his eyes to burn. At each sound, Billy would glance at the kennel expecting the beast to come roaring out.

He did this EVERY day.

The dog waited patiently, gnawing at the corner of its bone. It enjoyed this game. It chuckled to itself each time the boy leapt in panic, getting ready to run at the sound of her growl. What fun this was! She knew all she had to do was wait then it would be time. The dog took a long, loud lick of the bone's length whilst starring deliberately at one of his legs. She made sure it was a moment when he was looking at her. Oh, what delicious fun this was!

It did this every day.

Billy took his eyes off the dog. He was sure it had been licking its lips whilst staring at his leg. A fearful shiver went down his spine as the sun reflected off the dog's white teeth. He was beginning to get close to the kennel. This was the danger time. The palms of his hands were moist and clammy and he was starting to find it difficult to keep hold of the trowel, to keep it from slipping to the ground and into a pile of repugnant poo. He tried to wipe the sweat from his hands onto his jeans but too soon they were damp and slippery again. His face felt hot and stuffy under the scarf; perspiration was trickling into his eyes, blurring his vision. Why didn't the dog just attack? Why did it torture him like this? He just wanted it all to be over.

Inch by inch, Billy moved towards the kennel scooping. Inch by inch he cleared the ground of the foul light and dark brown patches. Inch by inch, he shuffled towards the dog's jaws. Until, he was so close he could feel the dog's warm breath stroking the hairs of his bare skin. His heart seemed to fill his chest, pounding so loud to obliterate all sound.

Snap! The dog leapt forward in a blur of motion. **Snap!** Its jaws just missing Billy's arm. Billy scrambled backwards, away from the beast, skidding slightly on a brown pile as he sped frantically towards the safety of the house.

Cuddles settled comfortably back down in her kennel. She licked her bone and chuckled to herself. It was such a good game!

Billy turned the key hard in the lock, pulling on the door's handle to check it was locked. He kicked his shoes off, removed the scarf from his lower face, placed the trowel in a bag under the stairs and dumped the now filled plastic bag in the bin in the front garden. Closing the door, he stood in the hallway and took in some deep breaths of air and began to shake uncontrollably.

In the evening, he had to **feed the dog!**

HE DID THIS EVERY DAY. Except Wednesdays.

WEDNESDAY

Billy trudged up the hill after school. The rain pounded down onto the pavement and his sodden head. It would have been nice to have a new coat that fitted, one that could keep the rain off. But no. Mrs Slurb had spent the money on a little leather jacket (with matching briefcase) for the dog. How he hated that dog. The unseen ball of hate swelled another inch just at the thought of the creature.

Usually on reaching the front door, Billy's back would stiffen for what would have lain ahead. There would have been no escape from it. Day after day, the same thing usually awaited him on his return. Cuddles. That spiteful dog. That dark descendent of Cerberus. It would have been waiting for him. So would his parents, spluttering commands from their armchair thrones.

But not today.

Today was different.

Today was **Wednesday.**

69

Billy entered the hallway, quickly dumped his bag and coat on the floor, passed through the silence to the kitchen. There he opened the fridge, got out his father's SUGARITE COKE, poured himself *a glass* (remembering to rub out the black-line showing how much was left and replacing it with his own new one). Then he quickly grabbed his mother's biscuit barrel, took *two chocolate biscuits* (remembering to break a few and mix them with the rest. She wasn't good with numbers).

Billy then took the drink and biscuits into the front room and sat on a chair. He just sat. He didn't *even* turn on the TV. He had just half an hour before he would have to leave. For the moment, he just sat nibbling at a biscuit slowly and taking the occasional little sip of drink. For the moment, he just sat bathing in the wonderful silence.

At 6pm, Billy strolled up to the top of his road, turned right and went pass the local bus station until he came to the corner of the road. There he stopped. He looked up at the sign which stated boldly **The Ferret & Trouser Leg**, sighed and pushed open the pub door.

Inside the pub, at the foot of a chair, Cuddles pricked up an ear and let out a low rumbling growl. The boy was here. Even over the din of the crowd chattering, glasses clinking and scraping chairs, she could hear him shuffling quietly in. How she hated that boy. He would spoil her lovely time with *her* wonderful parents. Cuddles pawed at Mrs Slurb's foot, gained her attention, and gave a look as if to ask, 'What's he doing here?'

'Now, now, Coo-coo. Is mummy's baby still hungry? That little lice can't be feeding you right. Have some more din-dins,' and she placed a large pie with curry sauce in front of the dog. Mrs Slurb turned her attention back to the enormous screen at the back of the pub with two figures stood below it.

Almost unnoticed, Billy joined the group at the large wooden table. He was very careful to choose a seat furthest away from the glaring dog munching on a pie. To his left sat: a small wizard with a scar and next to him a red and white stripped youth with glasses. To his right sat: a witch with an ill-fitting hat and then an enormous Viking with crooked horns. Finally, at the end of the table with a dog at their feet sat a bulbous woman in red with a golden whip (who looked remarkably like Mrs Slurb) and a man in blue lycra with a poorly scrawled **S** on his chest (who looked remarkably like Mr Slurb). Littered around the grimy pub were other people in similarly odd outfits. Billy knew this was not fancy dress. This was **Darts' Nite**!

The skilled opponents battled it out on the board beneath the screen. The crowd looked on almost silent except for the odd chorus of 'One hundred and eighty!' and 'Bully – bully!' Then total hush returned except for the odd clink of a glass and the crunching of crisps. Then it was over. The audience responded with a clatter of noise as they rushed to the bar and toilets.

Mr Slurb returned to the table laden with drinks.

'Here you go, Tiny,' said Mr Slurb, passing the enormous Viking, with no neck, a jug of beer.

The tray of drinks dwindled down to nothing. Everyone at the table had been given a drink: the wizard, the witch, the spectacled-lad and the superheroes. Everyone, that is, except Billy. He hadn't *even* been given a glass of water.

'Ah, my poor baby's been forgotten,' said Mrs Slurb and she left the throng at the table to go to the bar. She waddled back into view, glass in hand, and poured it into a dish for the dog. 'How could daddy forget you?'

Cuddles farted appreciatively.

'Well done, Cuddles. That show's a good digestion, that does. And breeding. Better out than in, that's what I always say. Don't want to do yourself any harm,' and to prove his point, Mr Slurb belched loudly.

The table of people chuckled approval. All that is, except the invisible boy at the end who sat silently, digging his nails into his legs as the great hate ball inside him swelled.

'Table eigh-teen! Table eigh-teen!' screeched the barmaid over the heads of some elves sat at the bar.

'Here,' called Tiny, beckoning with his great wing-flapping arm.

The barmaid paced again and again between their table and the kitchen carrying plate after plate after plate of food before dropping a mound of cutlery in the middle of the table. The food was passed along the table to everyone. Mr Slurb looked down at his two large pies and poured curry sauce over the top before decorating it with a mound of greasy chips. Mrs Slurb arranged her greasy chips on her two pies before pouring the curry sauce all around. Cuddles sat at their feet devouring her two pies and curry sauce. And Billy stared down at nothing. Just wood. Just the table. Nothing else.

'Don't you start any of your whining,' said Mr Slurb, jabbing a plastic fork in Billy's direction. 'I'm not paying good money for a kid's meal only for you not to eat half of it. Besides it's not worth the money. I got you this instead.'

A packet of CHEEZO crisps and a ketchup sachet landed in front of Billy. This was *his* dinner. The hate ball inside him swelled larger.

'Kids nowadays are spoilt. Aren't they, Tiny?' commented Mrs Slurb with a mouth full of chips.

Tiny grunted in agreement and shovelled another piece of pie in his mouth. Mr Slurb smiled at his wife with a grin of chewed pie and sauce. Below them, on the floor, Cuddles snuffled her way through her second pie.

Billy pulled open the packet of CHEEZOs and ate slowly, deciding to skip the ketchup. The noise around him rose like a needle of joy as the next two darts' players started their match. This was Wednesday. This was Billy's best day of the week.

THE UPRISING

When Billy arrived home from school, he found the house in uproar. He sensed something was wrong when he entered the front room and found the armchairs empty and the television off! This just **never** happened. Puzzled, Billy returned to the hallway and took off his coat. A terrible wailing came from upstairs that sounded like his mother. There was definitely something dreadfully wrong in the Slurb household.

Billy's first thought was to hide or run from the house, only to show himself when everything had calmed down. Life had taught him that his parents *only* ever shrieked or shouted when he had done something wrong. And they found many things *he did* wrong.

But this seemed different.

So instead, he stayed rooted to the spot in the hallway. Glued there by a mixture of curiosity and dread.

At first, Billy couldn't spot the difference over the screams and wails of Mrs Slurb and the shouts of Mr Slurb. Then gradually, bit by bit, the difference revealed itself.

There was *no growl* from the dog.

There was *no yell* of, 'Come here, you horrible little maggot!'

There was *no screech* of, 'You wicked leech!'

Then came an ear-drum busting scream from Mrs Slurb. 'Oh, my baby! My poor baby!' She was definitely **not** on about Billy.

Safe in this wonderful knowledge, Billy climbed the stairs to investigate.

The dreadful noise was all coming from *his room!* So he pushed open the door to discover a shocking scene. Mrs Slurb was crammed on Billy's tiny bed cuddling a *very* quiet Cuddles who was *in* his (Billy's) tiny bed, all looked down upon by Mr Slurb clutching a grubby large towel in one hand and a can of aerosol in the other.

Before Billy could protest about *the dog* being given *his* bed, Mrs Slurb glared at him and said, 'This is all your fault, you ringworm. You haven't been feeding Cuddles properly. You haven't been looking after her right. If anything happens to her...'

'What's wrong?' asked Billy. Although he hated the beast, he couldn't help feeling sorry for any living thing in pain. Besides, if the dog died, his life would be **HELL.**

'You know, you eel. You know what you've done,' said Mr Slurb with venom.

Billy was mystified. Nothing his parents had said had made anything clearer as to what was wrong with the dog and what he had supposedly done. Billy was about to ask if they should phone the vets to help the poor, unfortunate animal when Cuddles began whimpering and yelping.

'My poor baby!' cried Mrs Slurb.

'Will it never end?' cried Mr Slurb who hurriedly put the towel to his face.

Cuddles let out one more loud whimper. This was followed by a strange gurgling-hissing sound as if a steam iron was warming up. Then a slushy-whoosh of a washing

machine beginning to spin. Finally, it ended
with an earth-breaking thunderous **PARP** of
a crazed church organ. Billy's duvet seemed
to lift a foot off the bed with Mrs Slurb
clutching it. At the same time, the room
filled with a toxic perfume that almost
peeled the paper from Billy's walls with its
tales of pies and curry sauce.

Mr Slurb frantically wobbled around the
room, spraying the air-freshener in his other
hand until the can was empty. Then
defeated, he slumped to the floor in the
corner of the room. Meanwhile, Mrs Slurb
had her face buried deep into the duvet and
was wailing loudly.

Billy staggered backwards to his bedroom
door, his feet almost buckling underneath
him, partly due to the smell. But mainly due
to an uncontrollable urge, an uncontrollable
urge to laugh at them all. Tears began to fill
his eyes and he had to clamp his mouth shut
like a vice to stop himself. Wiping away the
tears, Billy looked at Mr Slurb slumped in
the corner like a great, befuddled hippo.

'Quite right. You should be crying. Look what you done to baby!' said a gasping Mrs Slurb.

Billy looked at her, lying there, cuddling her precious *baby* who was lying in *his* bed in *his* room. He knew things would never change. Mr and Mrs Slurb would **always** be the same. In that brief moment, dog and parent seemed to merge into one so that in perfect vision Billy could see his future. A future of meeting the needs of two wallowing beasts, fetching chicken.

'Quick!' said Mr Slurb at the sound of gurgling-hissing. 'Fetch another can from the kitchen!'

Mrs Slurb glanced briefly at Billy with accusing eyes then buried her head at the sound of a slushy-whoosh.

Ignoring the two parents, Billy went to his sock drawer, took the piece of wishbone and left the room, closing the door on the deafening noises within.

HUGS, CUDDLES AND PHOTOGRAPHS

Billy woke up in bed which was strange. It was strange for a number of reasons.

First, because there was no flatulent dog sharing it whilst trying to gnaw one of Billy's limbs.

Second, because he had gone asleep on the sofa after disappearing from the house. Billy had made himself scarce after failing to bring supplies of air fresheners to Mr Slurb despite his ever-increasing yells. He had known his parents would have been furious at his refusal to help and so had spent most of the evening wandering the streets until he thought it was safe enough to return home.

Next, because he had made a wish. He had held onto that bone so tightly until it dug into the flesh of his hand and he wished. He wished desperately for loving parents; parents that would love him no matter what;

parents that would love him, care for him and take care of his every need. He didn't need things, he needed love.

That night, on the sofa in the dark, Billy had surreal dreams of farting pies floating on a lake of bubbling curry sauce. Flying overhead were supermarket chickens on multi-coloured aerosols as if they were bizarre witches on brooms. Some were circling, some soaring, some diving – an elaborate aerial display of all the fragrances you could imagine. A collision of smells and colours.

But the *strangest* thing were the two parents at the end of the bed intently staring at him.

Mrs Slurb was dressed in a neat, pressed, black uniform with a pristine, white frilly-apron on top and was holding a tray of food. And what a tray of food it was! On it was a silver rack of perfect toast, next to three silver serving pots each containing a different jam and a little silver spoon. Next to those, were a silver teapot, milk jug and a delicate, little silver tea cup and saucer. Finally, there was a salt dish set, spoon and silver egg cup in which sat a delicately pale-blue egg.

Stranger still was Mr Slurb who was dressed in a smart, dark suit with sharp creases and pristine white-collared shirt and red tie. His face was mostly obscured by a huge camera and flash gun which was pointed directly at Billy.

'Time to sit up, darling, so you can have breakfast,' said Mrs Slurb sweetly.

It took a moment for Billy to react. He sat up obediently for the tray to be placed carefully on his lap.

'Hold it!' said Mr Slurb just as Billy reached for a piece of toast. 'I want to capture this moment for posterity,' and with that he sprang into action, snapping away like a crazed paparazzi, the flash repeatedly blinding Billy. Then it stopped.

The parents leant over Billy, each gave him a huge hug and planted a massive, wet kiss on his cheeks then left the room, leaving a stunned Billy in bed.

THE GALLERY

Billy stuffed his face with food and got dressed for the day ahead. Leaving his room, Billy passed picture frame after picture frame on the wall. There appeared not to be an inch of space wasted in that mosaic pattern of different sized and shaped frames. In fact, there were even a few frames fixed to the ceiling. This *new* Mr Slurb was certainly keen on photography!

It was then that Billy noticed a terrifying thing. A thing that filled his heart with dread, causing his stomach to churn. **Every** photo, no matter its size, shape or colour, every photo was a picture of Billy: Billy in his school uniform; Billy on the beach; Billy eating breakfast (that very morning!); and even Billy asleep (he spotted that one in the corner on the ceiling). Surely, there had to be a picture that wasn't Billy?

'Hurry up, sweetie. You'll be late for school!' came Mrs Slurb's voice from the hall.

Now, when Billy finally made it pass all the disturbing images to the hallway, he was glad to discover that his *new* parents now resembled something almost normal in appearance.

Gone was Mrs Slurb's maid outfit (what was that all about?) and instead she had on a sensible, long, grey coat. As well as a sensible, long, grey skirt and white shirt.

Gone too was the large camera in Mr Slurb's flabby hand. Instead, he was wearing a sensible, long, grey coat over his suit with a large briefcase in his hand.

Neither of them were doing anything that could be described as strange which was a **BIG** relief. After all, today Billy had school.

'Shall we get moving then, mate? We can't be late,' stated Mr Slurb with a friendly tussle of Billy's hair. With that, they all trooped out of the house.

Billy had just started the walk down the hill of his road, in the direction of his school, when Mr Slurb cried out, 'Where are you going?'

'Walking to school,' Billy replied quite puzzled.

'*Walk* to school? We don't walk!' said Mrs Slurb in astonishment. 'It's far too *dangerous* for you to walk to school. You might fall over or be killed by a runaway lorry or be kidnapped by pirates! We **never** walk. We go by car, silly.'

Billy thought that the chances of Mrs Slurb's dangers happening were very slim but still going by car would be a very nice change to the journey. Under the old Mr and Mrs Slurb he had *never* been driven to school. They had *never* taken him to school. In fact, the old Mr and Mrs Slurb didn't even know where Billy's school was!

The new Mr Slurb unlocked the high-vis, luminous-yellow car and the parents climbed in. Billy just stood on the pavement gawking at the ugly thing.

'Well, get in then, mate,' said Mr Slurb, chuckling at his son's strange behaviour.

Billy wrenched the heavy door open then clambered up into the back seats. He fastened the cumbersome, criss-crossing, racing-driver's seat belt with a loud clunk. This was not a car. This was more like a tank. He fully expected rocket launchers to come out of the boot when Mr Slurb started the thing. If not that, at least a couple of machine guns. He slammed the heavy door shut.

'All safely in? Then let's go,' said Mr Slurb and, after a quick glance round at Billy's seatbelt, turned the key in the ignition.

The great car growled into life like a slowly stirring bear. Every bone in Billy's body shook at the roar of the engine as the car accelerated forward and down the hill.

'Oh, how I love this car. Much better than our last one. It keeps us all so much safer,' said Mrs Slurb. 'Especially our little angel in the back.'

'That's right,' added Mr Slurb. 'Of course, it needed just a few changes to make it *really* safe: triple bull-bars (front and back), armoured plating, bullet-proof glass, air filtration system...'

'And the siren? You've remembered to add a siren?!' wailed Mrs Slurb suddenly alarmed.

'Yes, of course, darling. And pop-up flashing lights hidden in the bonnet. We can't be too careful,' said Mr Slurb in his most reassuring voice.

'Oh, thank heavens. Just anything could happen to our little boy if we broke down and didn't have those.'

Billy sat in the back of the car listening to all this as the rows of houses went by the window. He was beginning to think he had made a mistake. These new parents seemed *just* a little bit barmy and his wish *might* not work out quite how he had imagined. Unfortunately, in his haste to get dressed, he had left the wishbone behind in the bedroom. Besides, he had never used the wishbone before during daylight so didn't know what would happen. He had no choice but to see the day through and hope things didn't get any stranger.

DANGER DANGER

Mr Slurb was *not* a happy man. This had been made very clear by the loud string of exotic phrases he had yelled while hitting the car's dashboard. Let's just say, they are far too rude to write here or utter aloud in front of your mother. They would make any person's eyebrows curl and ears explode.

The cause of this unhappiness was the search for a parking space very near to Billy's school. The huge tank of a car was just too big for any of the remaining spaces and there weren't too many as everyone seemed to have exactly the same idea about driving there. *And* the Head Teacher wouldn't let him park in front of the school for some Health and Safety reason. *And* they had had to park a couple of streets away from the school, just around the corner from where they lived.

'If it wasn't for that daft Head Teacher and her rules, we wouldn't have to do this.

Making us risk our little angel's life. What is she thinking?' despaired Mrs Slurb.

'Just she wait until the next School Governor's Meeting. We'll show her,' stated Mr Slurb with menace. 'Being Governor's at the school should count for something!'

'You're Governors?' said Billy astonished. The other Slurb parents would **never** have given up time to be away from the telly and food.

'Of course, we are. We have to make sure *our* precious angel gets the very best of care and attention,' stated Mrs Slurb.

'Right, everyone, be on your guard,' said Mr Slurb switching off the engine. He then clambered out, slammed the door and made his way to the boot of the car.

Mrs Slurb leapt (surprisingly lightly for such a bulbous woman) from the car to the pavement. She kicked the door shut and immediately stood in a Karate-attack stance, eyeing any passer-by with suspicion. Finally, after struggling with the unfamiliar seat harness, Billy stepped from the car and shut the door.

'Ok, my precious, quickly to Mr Slurb!' said Mrs Slurb with urgency. 'It's time to kit up!'

Billy calmly strolled to the rear of the car where Mr Slurb became a sudden blur of action. First, he grabbed from the boot American footballer shoulder pads and shoved these on Billy before he could protest. Then came knee pads, shin guards, elbow pads, wicket keeper gloves and a riot helmet with face guard. This was all topped off with a high-vis, bright pink jacket. Mr Slurb then grabbed a utility belt with all kinds of gadgets (surely that wasn't CS gas, a taser gun and pepper spray?) as well as a round riot shield. He urgently put these on himself. Finally, satisfied Billy was as protected as he could be, Mr Slurb slammed the boot shut.

Billy stood almost unable to move under all that padding and equipment. Mr Slurb suddenly grabbed him with one arm and gave Billy a huge hug. 'Ready then, my precious?'

said Mr Slurb looking Billy earnestly in the eyes.

Billy tried to nod in the helmet but his head barely moved.

'Then let's go,' and with that they set off on their journey of two streets to the school. Mr Slurb led at the front, shield at the ready; Billy waddling in the middle underneath padding and helmet; Mrs Slurb taking up the rear in Karate mode.

SCHOOL FRIENDS

You will be pleased to know, Billy did not fall over on the way to school. Nor did he get killed by a runaway lorry. And he certainly wasn't kidnapped by pirates. In fact, it was a walk to school like many other children do week after week where **nothing** at all of interest happens. Well, almost.

As Billy neared the front gate of the school, the other children and parents couldn't help but notice the strange trio heading that way. At first, it was one or two stifled giggles. Then, some splutters and coughs until they gathered together and grew momentum like a hovering storm and became a flood of laughter, yells and openly pointing fingers. Billy just wanted the pavement to open up and suck him down, there and then.

'Is this all really necessary, Mr and Mrs Slurb?' asked the Head Teacher as she stood at the gate. She looked down at Billy with obvious sympathy.

'Of course, it is. Why wouldn't it be?' demanded a rather defensive Mrs Slurb.

'Don't you think it's going just a little bit far, a little bit too protective?' she suggested mildly.

'Too much? Nonsense!' said Mr Slurb, shocked at such a crazy notion.

'It's just that...it's just that it's *extremely* unlikely anything would happen to him on the way to school,' said the Head.

'Now, you listen here. Just because *this* lot...' said Mrs Slurb, randomly jabbing her finger at parents, '...don't love their children and don't look after them right and don't want to keep them safe but leaving them heading towards danger doesn't mean *we* have to do the same.' And with that, Mrs Slurb pushed pass the Head Teacher, pulling Billy by the arm, followed by an extremely indignant Mr Slurb.

At the door to Billy's classroom, Mr Slurb removed the riot helmet, jacket and padding from Billy. Then he gave Billy a very tearful hug and a big, wet kiss on the cheek.

'Oh, how I hate this part of the day. You be careful, now. Be on your guard. Don't run and remember to only wash your hands with this,' said Mr Slurb, taking a small container of ULTRAGUARD ANTI-BACTERIAL HANDWASH from his utility belt and handing it to Billy.

'Don't worry, my precious one,' said Mrs Slurb, giving Billy an equally tearful hug and an enormous, sloppy kiss. 'You'll be seeing both of us very soon so don't worry. You enjoy your day. And be careful.' Mrs Slurb finally dragged herself away from her precious angel, her whole body shaking with great sobs.

Billy was grateful to get in the classroom away from that Mr and Mrs Slurb, not to mention all the giggles and laughter of other parents and children. This was just dreadful. How could such a simple wish go so terribly wrong? He would just have to get on with the school day, try to ignore the jokes and comments from other children, and then use the wishbone when he got home. At least in here, in the classroom, he was free from those parents.

The teacher entered the classroom, the sniggers and remarks died down to nothing. The class quickly sat at their tables (not surprisingly, no one chose to sit next to Billy) and the teacher clicked a button on the computer on her grey desk. She gave a warning glance at the faces in the room, and took the register. All was as it should be.

Billy breathed a sigh of relief. All at once, there was a scuffling noise behind him, a scraping of chairs and a large, grey form sat down in the empty chair beside him. The long grey coat was gone but a clip-on school tie had been added to the white shirt instead.

'It's ok, Billy, I'm here to help you,' said Mrs Slurb as she reassuringly patted one of his hands.

Billy groaned. Then, out of nowhere, a face he recognised appeared at the classroom window, small digital camera in hand, snapping away in a bid to *capture every moment* for posterity. Billy groaned again. Louder.

'Mrs Slurb,' said the teacher, struggling to contain the fiery furnace inside, 'have we not discussed how it is inappropriate for you to sit next to Billy in school? Have we not talked about how, in fact, you are too old for this school?'

There was a slight bang on the window from Mr Slurb as he juggled to control the two cameras he now held in his hands in order to better capture this moment between mother and son. The teacher's left eyebrow began to twitch like a caterpillar on a string.

'Yes, Miss Grandrecul. However, as you know, education is so very important for **everyone**. It is important we all continue to learn no matter our ages so I thought it wouldn't harm me to go back to school. After all, things have changed so much. And I might even enjoy it,' said Mrs Slurb with a sweet smile.

The teacher's mouth began to twitch. There was a clunk at the window as Mr Slurb now tried to balance a third camera between the other two and press the shutter buttons with his nose. Billy groaned and hid his face in his hands.

'Oh no, sweetie. Aren't you well?' asked Mrs Slurb, full of grave concern.

Billy watched as the teacher took decisive action. Now with head twitching, she crossed the room to a large, red button fixed to the wall. On it was a single word written in black permanent pen: **SLURB**. She hit it forcefully with her fist. All at once, in every corridor of the school, outside every room and on every staircase, piercing alarms sounded. The shock of the noise made Billy leap out of his skin. The pounding of footsteps could just be heard coming from outside the room and then two burly figures stood at the classroom door. Their black uniforms simply stated: SLURB SQUAD.

'Kindly remove her!' said the teacher, her hand violently twitching as she pointed at Mrs Slurb.

The two uniforms sprang into action; their hands grabbing Mrs Slurb by the arms and frog-marching her forcefully out the door. There was a clatter at the window as Mr Slurb dropped his cameras at the excitement of capturing such a wonderful moment between teacher, mother and son. That was one definitely for pride of place in the front room. Perhaps above the fireplace? Poster sized?

'Right, now, class,' said the teacher as she lowered the shutters over the window and doors, 'English.'

The rest of the day was almost like any other day at school like many other children have week after week. Billy sat obediently through lessons and did his work. He joined in with football matches at playtime and ate his splodge of a school dinner in the school canteen. He also ignored the cries from his parents on the other side of the school fence with the two Slurb Squad members watching them closely (Mr Slurb still with a camera in hand).

Billy knew all he had to do was rush home, grab the bone, make a wish and all would be right. These parents would be out of his life forever.

The minutes to home-time seemed to tick pass particularly slowly for Billy. It was almost as if the clock had it in for him. Each tick taking longer than the last. Why wouldn't the school day come to an end? Get a move on. Come on. I need to get home. Tick. Click.

The home-bell sounded and Billy was out of the door before the teacher could react. He ran through the gate, swerved pass his two parents with arms out ready to greet him, and along the first street. Then down the next street, avoiding a lady with a buggy, and around the corner and up the hill to his house. Then key in lock, front door open, up the stairs pass the pictures to his bedroom. Breathing a huge sigh of relief, Billy pushed open the bedroom door and calmly went over to the small bedside cabinet to grab the wishbone. *The bone* was gone!

THE CHASE

Billy was rooted to the spot by disbelief. He just stood there, staring at the space on the bedside cabinet willing the wishbone to be there. He couldn't believe what had happened. Inside his mind screamed. Perhaps he had made a mistake. Perhaps he had not left it there. Memories can be tricky things making you believe something is real when it's not.

Billy forced himself to be calm despite his racing heart. Think! What had he done that morning? He had breakfast in bed!

Billy checked the bed. Nothing.

Then what? He had got dressed for school!

Billy checked his pyjamas and uniform pockets. Nothing.

Then, before leaving the room? He had thrown the wishbone onto the cabinet and gone downstairs! Nothing. In the drawer? Nothing. On the floor by it? Nothing! **Nothing! NOTHING!** It had gone.

Billy heard the clunk of the front door and Mr and Mrs Slurb's voices. Perhaps they had seen it! He raced downstairs, almost crashing into the two stunned parents.

'Ah. So you've decided to greet us after all. What was all that rush...' said Mr Slurb.

'The bone? Have you seen the piece of wishbone?' Billy asked urgently.

'A wishbone? What on earth are you on about?' said Mrs Slurb, puzzled.

'A chicken's wishbone! I left it on the cabinet in my bedroom. Have you *seen it?*' Billy demanded desperately.

'A chicken wishbone? I don't think so. If I had, I would certainly have put it in the bin. Who wants a thing like that lying around the house, gathering germs? No, I would certainly have got rid of it,' she replied.

'Quite right,' Mr Slurb agreed.

'No!' cried Billy almost collapsing to the floor. The wishbone had been thrown in the rubbish. The wishbone was gone forever.

Billy went to the front door and swung it open watched by his stupefied parents. He knew it was useless, there was no hope. But he just couldn't believe it. That this was the end.

'Er, evening,' said a rather surprised man returning the bin he had just emptied into the lorry.

Billy was stunned. They had only just collected the rubbish. He had a chance! The wishbone was in the lorry and it was getting away! Billy sped after it, heart pounding, as it moved down the hill and turned. It was in the next street, stopping at houses on the way. What could he do? He couldn't just jump in the lorry. He'd be stopped. No good asking – too many questions. There was nothing for it: he would just have to follow it.

Billy knew where the lorry was heading. All the local lorries went to the same rubbish dump. The problem was losing *his* lorry. He had to keep an eye on it or he'll never get the wishbone. He had to see where the lorry dumped its load.

Street after street, house after house, Billy tracked the lorry. Not too close to make anyone suspicious. Not too far to lose sight of it. Street by street, he followed the lorry, repeating the number plate to himself. His feet ached; his legs ached; his heart ached. He *must* get that wishbone!

At last, the lorry pulled up at the gate leading to the dump and the gate guard let it in. All around the site was a high fence whose job it was to keep people out. Fortunately, it was no good at it. It was rusty, broken in places and never repaired. After all, who would want to steal rubbish?

Billy waited for the guard to go back into his little office then darted along to a gap in the fence, keeping an eye on the lorry. Quick in, he ducked down behind a stack of used paper. Peeking between the stacks, he spotted his lorry and watched as it picked a spot to dump its rubbish. Good. It was a distance from the guard house. Probably far enough away not to be spotted. He had to take the risk.

Heart pounding in his chest, senses on edge, Billy ran over squashed plastic bottles, yesterday's tissues and half-eaten food to where the lorry had been. Taking a deep breath, he gingerly began to move rubbish out of the way, piece by piece as the seagulls swooped overhead. Their screeched warnings sent Billy's heart into his mouth.

After twenty minutes, Billy no longer cared about the rancid smell of rotten food as it squelched between his fingers, under his nails. More and more frantically, he cast rubbish aside as the light above him dimmed. Twilight, soon it would be too dark to see. Where was it? Was it even here?

A seagull landed a few metres from him. Something had caught its eye and it was pecking at the rubbish trying to get at it. What had it seen? An awful feeling filled Billy's stomach. It was the bone. The gull was after the wishbone!

Billy clambered towards the bird, waving his arms and shouting. At first the bird took off but deciding the prize too great, returned. Skidding and sliding and crashing across the rubbish pile, Billy threw himself at the feet of the gull after the wishbone. Too late! The seagull had won its prize and took off. The wishbone was gone!

TRAPPED

Billy did not notice the yells and screams of the parents when the rubbish dump guard delivered him home to his house. Nor did he notice when Mrs Slurb fainted at the sight of the missing shoe and the rancid, food encrusted sock on his left foot. He did not even notice Mr Slurb set up his camera and tripod and take photographs of the event. And Billy certainly did not notice the five baths he was given with Mr and Mrs Slurb scrubbing away at him until his skin was raw. Billy only noticed when the light was switched off and he found himself in bed. Then he simply cried.

Billy woke exhausted. He did not feel any better. He was struck with these Slurb parents and there was nothing he could do. How he cursed the day he set eyes on that shop. He should have stuck with the old Slurbs and been grateful. At least with them, he had some peace at school. But with these: *there was no escape.*

Billy dragged himself from bed. No daft mother in a daft outfit with breakfast in bed for him or daft father with his stupid camera. Things were looking up. This was almost a normal start to the day.

Billy changed into his casual Saturday clothes and wondered if these parents would be having chicken for dinner. He almost cried at the thought. He flung open his bedroom door and stopped. He could go no further. There in front of him was a huge, domed, clear-plastic wall sealing him in to his room. At foot-height there was a rectangular slot, larger than a letterbox, and at waist height there was a bright-red door bell but *no way to get out.* No handle. No zip. Nothing. What was all this?

With nothing else to do, Billy pressed the bell. A few moments later, Mr and Mrs Slurb appeared on the other side of the plastic wall.

'Good morning,' said Mrs Slurb chirpily. 'How did you sleep? Well?'

'What is all this?' Billy asked, indicating the wall.

'This? This is for your own good, angel. It is to keep you safe.'

'And how do I get out?' Billy asked.

'Out?' said Mr Slurb, shocked at the suggestion. 'Why would we let you out? You wouldn't be safe then. Anything might happen to our precious angel.'

'But how am I meant to live? Eat? Go to the toilet?' Billy pleaded.

'Oh, we thought of that, silly. There's now a little toilet and shower in your cupboard...' said Mrs Slurb.

'And this is for your food,' said Mr Slurb, opening the overgrown letterbox and shoving through a breakfast tray by way of explanation.

'You'll be perfectly safe. We'll always know where you are and you won't be putting yourself in any danger. It's the perfect solution,' said Mrs Slurb, grinning happily.

'But...but this isn't right. It isn't normal...' Billy stuttered, looking from one parent to the other for any glimmer of reason.

'Now, now, Billy. You're beginning to sound like that daft Head Teacher of yours,' said Mr Slurb, chuckling.

This was crazy. No, this was beyond crazy. This was a hellish nightmare. No escape. He was to live a prisoner of his bedroom with only these two grinning idiots for company. *He had to escape.*

Filled with rage, rage at losing the bone, rage at making such a wish, rage at such foolish parents, Billy hurled himself at the great, plastic wall only to go bouncing off it, backwards onto the floor. That hurt. An intense pain shot through his left shoulder. He needed something sharp.

'I don't know what's gotten into him lately,' said a disapproving Mrs Slurb.

'It's just a phase,' said Mr Slurb as he snapped away with his camera.

Billy frantically rummaged through the breakfast things but without any luck. It

was all plastic. His wardrobe and cabinet –
perhaps in there. Billy yanked out the
cabinet drawer, emptying the contents on
the floor. Nothing of use. Just bits of old
pens and scribbled on pads. And in the
wardrobe, he found clothes, twisted coat
hangers, nothing else.

What if he threw something heavy? Maybe
not at the plastic, that wouldn't break. But
at the window. That was still glass and there
was a drainpipe next to it, just outside. *He
could escape that way!*

Billy picked up various small objects from
around the room: a boot, a large book, even
the cabinet drawer. They just weren't heavy
enough to break a window. He needed
something heavier. The bed? No, silly idea.
Far too big for a boy his size. What to use?

Then Billy spotted it. He went over to the
bedside cabinet and pulled. The cabinet
moved far more easily than he had expected
and so it crashed forward to the floor, just
missing Billy's toes.

It was then Billy saw it. It seemed to shimmer in the light as it lay there wedged between the skirting board and the wooden floor. It had been hidden by the cabinet. It was the piece of wishbone. He was sure it was *his* wishbone. Billy began tugging at it desperately but it didn't seem to want to budge.

'What's he found there? I can't quite make it out,' said Mr Slurb, lifting his head up from the camera.

'I'm not quite sure…I think it's a bone. **It's a dirty, germ covered bone!**' Mrs Slurb screamed in terror.

Billy turned his head, looked at the panicked Mr and Mrs Slurb, and began clawing at wood with his nails. Ignoring the splinters piercing his flesh, he tried to dig into the floor, to dig out the bone. It was no use.

'Quick! Get the nuts off the door. We must get in and save him!' screamed Mrs Slurb.

Mr Slurb dropped his camera and sped off to get his spanner. He had to save his son! He quickly returned and Billy could hear the squeaking of one of the nuts holding the door in place, then the sound of it hitting the floor.

'Hurry, Mr Slurb, hurry. Who knows what dreadful thing that bone can give him!' cried Mrs Slurb as she banged hopelessly at the door.

Another nut fell to the floor. Just two remained.

Billy looked at the floor boards. All he managed to do was turn his fingers into ten hedgehogs with wooden spines. What could he use? If he didn't find something quick all would be lost. Then it hit him just as the third nut clunked heavily down.

'Almost there, Mrs Slurb. He will soon be safe with us.'

A coat hanger! He should use one of the twisted coat hangers from the wardrobe! Billy sped to the wardrobe, grabbed a coat hanger and began using it to claw and pull at the wishbone. There was a clunk behind him. The last nut holding the door in place was removed. The parents grabbed the door and began pulling it from the bolts.

At last, the wishbone popped out and Billy picked it up and held it triumphantly like a trophy. He turned his head, looked at the panicked Mr and Mrs Slurb pulling at the great plastic door, and grinned.

'I wish,' said Billy smiling and taking a moment to think. 'I wish for parents. They don't have to be very sporty or very lazy. They don't have to love and care for me every moment of the day. They shouldn't hate and despise me. All I wish for, all I really wish for are two average, nothing special, nothing perfect parents that I can love and live with.'

FAREWELL

Billy turned the corner into Ringwald Road and waited for his mum and dad to catch up. He had won the race again. He had won the race to the bottom of his road the last three Saturdays as well. Billy suspected his dad was letting him win but he did not mind. It was part of the fun, both of them pretending it was a proper race and both of them knowing it wasn't.

Mr Slurb came around the corner doing exaggerated puffing. 'Looks like you beat me again,' he laughed.

'Afraid so, dad. I'll give you a chance, next time.'

'Oi, cheeky,' said Mr Slurb, ruffling Billy's hair.

Mrs Slurb caught them up and began a lot of exaggerated tutting. 'I don't know which one of you is worse. Haven't you grown out of such nonsense,' and she took Billy's left hand in hers.

Billy was about to take his dad's as well before going up the hill when he spotted the curious little shop on the corner. Much of the glass was still covered with faded black and white advertisements and the rest still needed a good wash.

'Hold on a second, mum and dad. I just need to go in there,' said Billy.

'Ok. We can wait a bit. Just don't be too long,' said Billy's mum.

'Yeh, it's our favourite tonight. Movie and a pizza,' added his dad.

Billy crossed over the road and pushed hard against the stiff door which swung open suddenly. Billy flew inside so quickly he almost crashed into the small man near the door.

'Sorry,' Billy spluttered.

The man smiled and went back to what he was doing. He was wearing very thick oven gloves whilst carrying a rather large, green egg towards one of the many shelves.

'Please excuse,' the small man said. 'This thing has a habit of bouncing away and burning anything it touches. Makes a marvellous pet when it hatches but most bothersome at this stage. And certainly not good to eat. Gives you terrible heartburn.'

Billy walked carefully around the man and headed towards the counter that seemed to be stacked high with old newspapers.

'Can I help you?' said the voice from behind the papers.

'Yes. I have this to give you,' said Billy, taking a wishbone from a zipped jacket pocket.

'Are you sure?' asked the voice. 'You know, these chicken bones are quite rare.'

'Yes, I'm quite sure,' said Billy, placing the wishbone on the counter.

A light-blue covered arm pushed aside some of the papers, sending them crashing to the floor, and the friendly face of the shopkeeper with the slightly-too-long beard smiled at Billy. 'Very well then.'

The shopkeeper took a dusty jar from beneath the counter, blew off the dust, popped off the lid, dropped in the wishbone and resealed the jar. He then took a large, brown paper label and wrote on it with a scratchy quill pen two simple words: **Wishbone (used).** The shopkeeper tied the label to the jar, then turned and place the jar on the shelf next to a large assortment of other jars, as well as boxes and tins.

'Thank you,' said Billy and turned and left the shop, avoiding the small man chasing an egg on the way out.

As Billy strolled up the hill to his house, holding one of each of his parents' hands, he took a quick glance back at the curious little corner shop. He was not surprised. It was gone.